DUNGZILLA

For
Larry, Joan,
Norman, Nancy
and Jojo.
Rosie Tinker is all of you.

James Foley makes children's books for children who read books. If you're a child and you're eating his books, you're doing it wrong. You might know his picture book *Stellarphant* or his graphic novel series *Secret Agent Mole*. He lives in Perth with his wife Renae, their two kids, and a labrador called Frankie. He's an ambassador for Books In Homes and Room To Read; a massive Marvel movie nerd; and comes from a long line of queuing enthusiasts.
Legend says James can grow a beard in an afternoon.

jamesfoley.com.au

DUNGZILLA

JAMES FOLEY

FREMANTLE PRESS

Greetings! I'm Sally Tinker, the world's foremost inventor under the age of twelve.

07 DAYS
SINCE LAST
JOE-TASTROPHE

And this strange specimen is my baby brother, Joe.
pick
pick
pick

Today, I'd like to reveal my latest and greatest invention.
The incredible ...
... the phenomenal, theEEARGH!!

Hi Sal!
How've you been?
CHARLI !!
clap clap clap clap clap
You know how I feel about hugs.
It's good to see you too.
And how's my little buddy?

Ladies and gentlemen - my colleague, Charli Stevenson. The world's foremost biologist under the age of eleven.
Who you talkin' to, Sal?
Oh, it's, uh ... nevermind.

*NB: artist impression only

Ladybugs?
No, they're beetles too, not bugs. And they're not all ladies either ...
Why am I holding a beetle, Charli?
Sorry, yeah. So anyway ...
This guy here is a very special kind of beetle. He's a **Scarabaeus sacer** - a sacred scarab - also known as ...

SCARABAEUS SACER
(Linnaeus, 1758)
• AKA sacred scarab / Egyptian dung beetle
• Eats dung
• Rolls dung
• Just really, really loves dung
• Able to fly
Tibial 'teeth' – used to dig tunnels and also to shape dung into balls
Eyes – dung beetles use the position of celestial objects to navigate. It's like a built-in GPS (Global Poo-sitioning System)
Pronotum – hard shell that protects the thorax. Think of it as armour worn by a tiny six-legged knight who rides a dungball instead of a horse
... the Egyptian dung beetle.
Uh, 'dung' beetle?

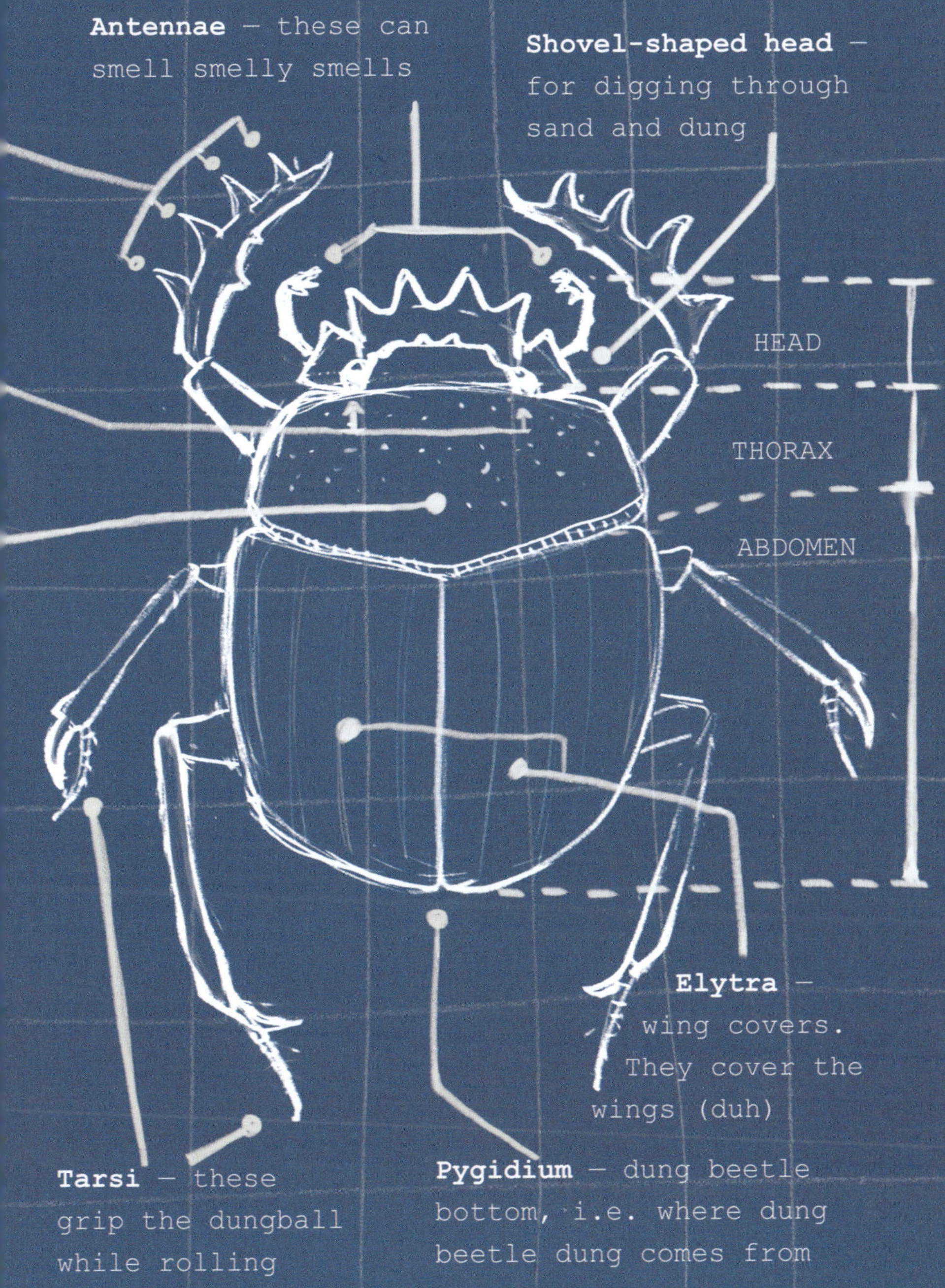

DID YOU KNOW? The ancient Egyptians worshipped a god called Khepri, who they believed had a dung beetle for a head.

Yep, a dung beetle.
His name's Douglas.
Dung as in ...
animal droppings?
Yep, dung as in
animal droppings,
also known as ...

manure
guano
spraints
scat

fewmets
frass
cowpats
pasture pastries
cow pies
and
meadow muffins

Dung beetles eat all kinds of dung. That's why they're called dung beetles.
Charli, EWWWW! Get this mucky monstrosity off me!

They're not monstrosities, Sal, they're actually really important.
Dung beetles get rid of heaps of dung every day - literally. If it wasn't for Douglas and his rellies, we'd all be up to our eyebrows in poop.
These little guys are unsung heroes.
Ooh! And check this out!
click
BZZZZZZZ

BZZZZZZ
EEEEK!!
The filthy freak of nature can fly!
BZZZZZZZZZ
He's caught a whiff of something. I don't see any dung around here though, so what's he smelling?
I'll give you one guess.

BZZZZZZZZZZZZZZZZZZZ
HAHA! Whoops.
Now you've got me thinking, Sal ...

ZZZZ...
BZZZZZZZZZZZZZZZZZ
Gotcha!
... why don't you use a bunch of dung beetles to clean Joe's nappies?
Not while he's wearing them, of course.

It'd be an all-natural, environmentally friendly solution!
Charli, could we save this delightful topic of conversation for another time? I need to run a test of my latest invention.
Wow! So ... it blows up balloons?
What? No, it's a matter magnitude manipulation machine.
It can scale items to immense or infinitesimal proportions.

Behold ...
the world's first
atomic inflation/deflation
engine!
Joe, don't
touch that.
SMACK
It makes
things really big
or really small.

Decorative cables
Vacuum-sealed embiggetron storage ring
Nuclear power source (don't tell Mum)
Control panel (see REAR VIEW for details)
Optional cup holder
Resize factor control unit
Vacuum-sealed shrinkatron storage ring
It's a growth ray AND a shrink ray?
Correct. I call it the Resizenator.

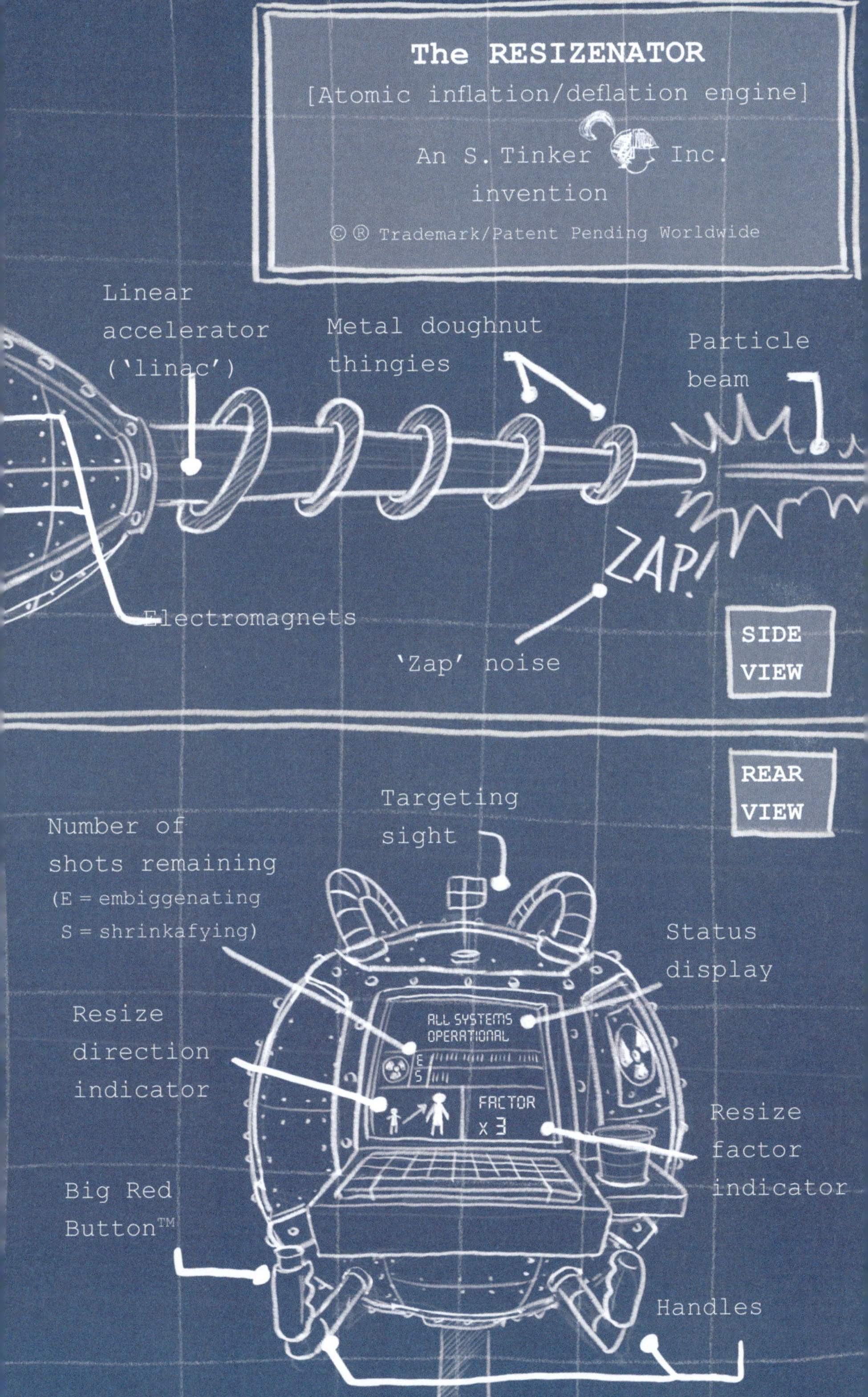
The RESIZENATOR
[Atomic inflation/deflation engine]
An S. Tinker Inc. invention
© ® Trademark/Patent Pending Worldwide
Linear accelerator ('linac')
Metal doughnut thingies
Particle beam
ZAP!
Electromagnets
'Zap' noise
SIDE VIEW
REAR VIEW
Targeting sight
Number of shots remaining
(E = embiggenating
S = shrinkafying)
Status display
ALL SYSTEMS OPERATIONAL
E
S
Resize direction indicator
FACTOR
x 3
Resize factor indicator
Big Red Button™
Handles

It runs on two new types of subatomic particle that I discovered: the **embiggetron** and the **shrinkatron**.
atom
embiggetron
shrinkatron
I observed that if I bombarded an object with a beam of concentrated, accelerated embiggetrons, I could increase the size of that object proportionally.
Shrinkatrons have the opposite effect. As a matter of fact, I used them to shrink the tools in Brobot's forearms.*
But how is any of this even possible?

*see 'Brobot'

I honestly have no idea. But I'm Sally Tinker! I will not be beholden to the laws of physics.

Well, is it safe? I don't know if you should be playing around with this if you don't know how it works ...
Oh, come now, Charli, the risks are worth it ...

With my Resizenator, we could turn tiny model houses into full-sized dwellings in seconds, eliminating homelessness.
We could send miniaturised supplies to disaster areas, and re-enlarge them as required.
We could create a microscopic submersible craft capable of navigating the interior of the human body!

Marvel as I turn this small pizza into ...
clap
clap
clap

Wow, that sounds fantastic!
Indeed - it would be quite a voyage. Probably enough adventure to fill a whole book*.
*see 'Gastronauts'
But for now, I have something else in mind.
... a LARGE PIZZA!

Resize factor set to 'x 3'. Initiating test.
EMBIGGENATING SEQUENCE ACTIVATED.
... FIRING IN 3 ...
Charli, where's Joe?
JOE, NO!
1 ...
MALFUNCTION!
ABORT DENIED
Have a nice day
FACTOR
x 3
MALFUNCTION!
ABORT DENIED
Have a nice day
FACTOR
x 300

TARGET ACQUIRED.
2 ...
Douglas!
BZZZZZZZZZZZZZ
Abort!
... FIRE.
BZZZZZZZZZ
We're too la--

ABORT DENIED
FACTOR
X 300
Nothing happened.
But where's Joe?!
And where's Douglas?
ABORT DENIED
FACTOR
X 300

Joe!
Douglas!!

Thank the Higgs boson! He's OK.
He must have sat down a nanosecond before the beam fired.

Hmmm, that's curious - the beam hit Douglas and the pizza slice, so why haven't they changed size??
Hey, little guy!

Thought you'd have another go at Joe's nappy, did ya? Your appetite is gonna get us in trouble one day.
SHOOOP
Doug's always hungry. He's a growing boy!
Isn't that right, Dougie? Isn't that --
-- uh, Sal?
RUN!

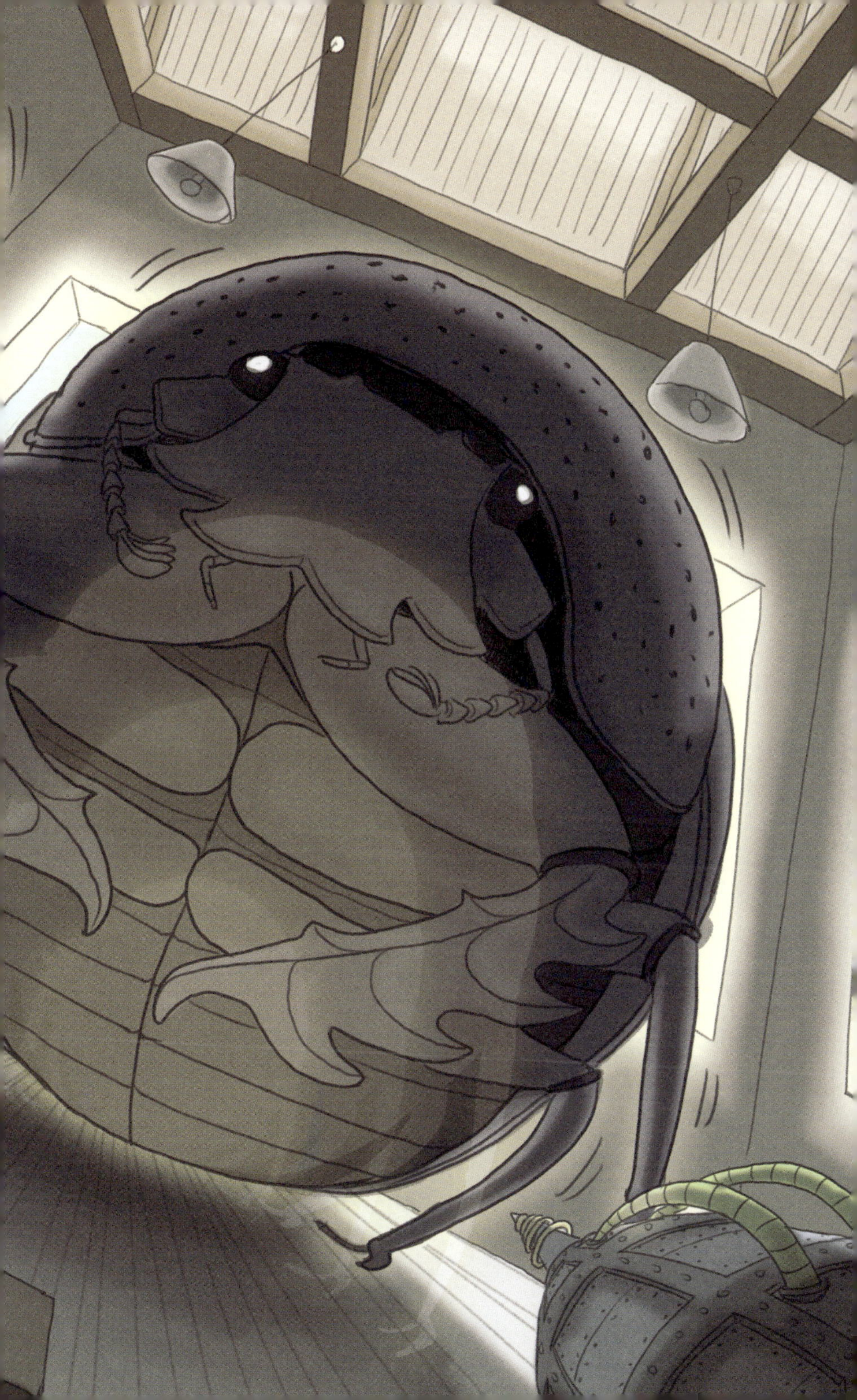

creeeakk...
S. TINKER INC.
STOP

BOOM
S. TINKE
INC
STOP

STOP
WHUMP
*cough
cough
cough*

BZZ
COME BACK!
This is a disaster ...
Oh, right. Your lab.
Sorry Sal! I'm just worried about Douglas. He's my responsibility.

TINKER AUTO
DOUGLAS!
DOUGLASSS!!
ZZZZZZzzzz
I know! He's going to miss lunch.
No, Charli - he's OUR responsibility now. We'll sort this out together.

Luckily the Resizenator seems to be functioning. But what went wrong before? I specifically set the resize factor to x 3 ...
wipe wipe

MALFUNCTION!
ABORT DENIED
Have a nice day
FACTOR
X 300
x 300 ?
Why does this
say x 300 ?!
GRRRRR!!
JOE! What have
I told you about hiding
food in my inventions!

It appears Joe's snack caused the Resize Factor Control Unit to short out.
But it's fixed now, right? We can shrink Douglas back?
All systems are operational. However ... we only have four shots of shrinkafying ray.
Will four shots be enough?

We only need to zap Douglas once. So assuming we can locate him, it should be fine.
Well ... can we collect more shrinkatrons, just to be safe?
Sorry, no. It's the PLOT Device, you see.
The 'PLOT Device'?
Yes. That box over there. Let me show you ...
... the Particle eLectromagnetic Orbital Trajectory Device. 'PLOT Device' for short.

I used it to create the embiggetrons and shrinkatrons. Unfortunately, it's suffered serious damage and will take days to repair.

We'll just have to make do with our four shots of shrinkafying ray.
In fact, it will only be three shots ...

... we'll use one to make sure the Resizenator still works. Charli, can you grab Joe? He's in the blast zone. AGAIN.
Sure, Sal.
C'mon, Joe.
Pizza time's over, OK?
eep!
SNAP

Initiating test.
SHRINKAFYING SEQUENCE ACTIVATED.
... FIRE.
ZAP
Success!

TARGET ACQUIRED.
FIRING IN 3 ... 2 ... 1 ...
PING!
Sally Louisa Tinker!
SPLATCH
TINKER AUTO
SCREECH

Uh, hi Nan.
Hi Ms Tinker.
What in the blue blazes happened this time?!
And how am I gonna explain this to your mum?

Folks, meet my maternal grandmother, Rosie Tinker: auto mechanic, ex-race car driver, ex-stunt pilot, ex-a few other things she says I don't have the clearance to know about yet.
This is worse than that time with the robot.
Even worse than the time you made a life-size 'model' volcano for the science fair - we still haven't got the magma out of the carpet.
Even worse than the time your miniature black hole escaped from its enclosure and ate the neighbour's cat.

Sorry Nan, we, uh, accidentally embiggened Charli's dung beetle. But we can reduce him. We have the technology. We just need someone to drive us to wherever he's got to.
Riiiight, so ...
... you two made a Dungzilla ...
... and now you want me to join your dangerous and foolish mission ...
... a mission that will surely involve high-speed driving and threats to life and limb?

Correct.
Then count me in!
Just don't tell your mum.
Thanks, Nan. I'll load up the Resizenator, then we can search for Douglas.
Sounds like a plan. Shouldn't be too hard to find a giant dung beetle.
I hope you're right.

Douglas will be so confused, and lonely, and hungry ...
He's hungry?
He's hungry! Eureka! I know where Douglas is going.
We last saw him flying west, correct?
Yep.
And he only eats dung, correct?
Uh huh ...
So where would a giant dung beetle find enough dung to satisfy his enormous appetite? Somewhere west of here ...
Oh. Oh no.
Oh yes ...

'... the Eaton Squats Sewage Farm'.
EATON SQUATS

HELLO MY NAME IS
MR EATON
The World's #2 Sewage Farmer
BZZZZZZZZZ
HELLO MY NAME IS
MR EATON
The World's #2 Sewage Farmer
BZZZZZZZ
ZZZZZ
MR EATON
The World's #2 Sewage
BZZZZZZZZ

ZZZZZ
BZZZZZ
AAAAAAA

Meanwhile ...
Sally, I need to tell you something.
There are three kinds of dung beetle. There're the dwellers, who live in dung pats.
Then there're the tunnelers, who live under dungpats.
Is this important, Charli?
This is super important, trust me!

Douglas is the third kind; the most famous kind ...
... he's --
AAAAAA
SCREEECH!
AAAAAAAAAAAAAAAAAAAA

That's Mr Eaton. He's traumatised!
I would be too if I worked at a sewage farm.
AAAAAAAAAAAAAAAAAAAA
RUMBLE
What was that?!
It's what I was trying to tell you!
Douglas isn't a dweller or a tunneller. He's a roller.
So if he's already at the sewage farm, he'll be heading this way any minute with a massive, ginormous ...

EATON
SQUATS

RUMBLE
... dungball.

That is one big ball of poop.
TINKER-AUTO
I've seen bigger.
RUMBLE

Hold on, kidlets!
SCREEECH
TINKER-AUTO

SHRINKAFYING SEQUENCE ACTIVATED.
TARGET ACQUIRED.
CRUNCH

The dungball is blocking the shot!
So let's shrink the dungball first.
Initiating!
FIRING IN 3 ...
CRRRRKKKKKK
2 ...
CRACK
1 ...
... FIRE.
WHOA!!
ZAP

SHOONK!

I missed! Keep it steady, Nan!
Well, warn us next time there's a hazard ahead.
Sorry Sal, couldn't be helped.
Righto ...
Plink!
TINKER-AUTO

... there's a hazard ahead.
EEEEP!

WHUMP

All OK back there?
We're fine, Ms Tinker - at least, until Douglas catches up.
CREEEEAK

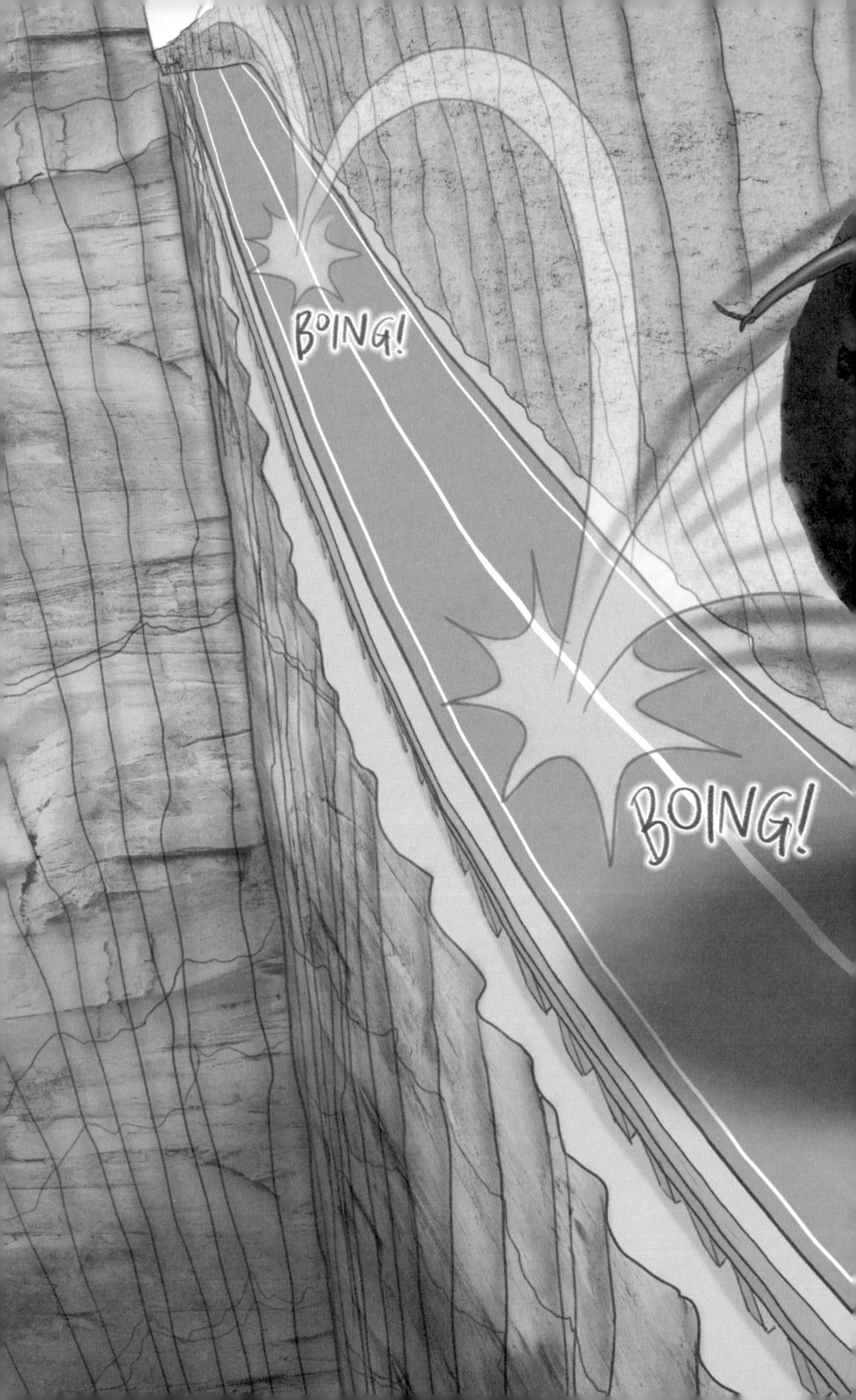
BOING!
BOING!

BOING!

BOING!

Whoa!!
SCREECH!!
BOING!
That was enough to make one micturate.
Yeah, or even pee a little.

Girls, Dungzilla's fallen behind.
Want me to reverse?
That's a negative, Nan.
He's coming to us!
BOING!

SHRINKAFYING SEQUENCE ACTIVATED. ACQUIRING TARGET ...
Is he in range, Sal?
Almost there ...

TARGET ACQUIRED.
Good boy, Dougie. Aunty Sal's gonna make it all better. I promise this won't hurt a bit.

It won't hurt, will it?
Not at all. Unless, on the off chance, he implodes. But even then it would be over nearly instantaneously, so no need to worry.
FIRING IN 3 ...
2 ...
1 ...
CLICK!

BZZZZZ
ZAP

ZZZZZ
... FIRE.

BZZZZZZ
We missed!

BOING!

BOING!
CRACK

CRUMBLE

NAN,
WATCH OUT!!

BZZZZZZZZ
BOING!
SCREEECH!

BZZZZZZzz
Blast!
We lost him ...
Poor Douglas! He looked so stressed.

Charli, what's Douglas's next move?

Well, once he catches the dungball and starts rolling it again, he'll look for a good spot to bury it. I'm guessing somewhere with open space and soft soil.
OK. Let's check the Holo-Map ...

Littleton Plateaus
Eaton Squats Sewage Farm
YOU ARE HERE
Plateaus Cave
... assuming he follows the road, the nearest open space is the park opposite home. Archimedes wept!
He's gonna destroy half the town and turn our front yard into a toilet.

Holo-Map
of Littleton and surrounds
An S. Tinker Inc.
invention
© ® Trademark/Patent Pending Worldwide
Runn Forest
CALCULATING DOUGLAS'S ROUTE ...
Ovadah Hill
LITTLETON
Slipson Falls
S.Tinker Inc. HQ
Lord Sproxton Park
DUNGBALL BURIAL ZONE
PROBABILITY = 123.45%

We have to get past these rocks.
The truck can't drive over boulders.
I didn't say we needed to drive.
We only have one shot of shrinkafying ray left, correct?
Yep.
But, we still have multiple shots of embiggenating ray ...
Why are you looking at me like that?

Charli, how would you feel about being bombarded with a beam of embiggetrons?
blink blink
I want to zap you with the Resizenator and make you big.
What?? Why?
An embiggenated human could easily lift the truck over the rocks and get us to Douglas.
Now, it can't be me because I need to operate the Resizenator.
And it can't be Nan because she needs to drive the truck.
And it can't be Joe because, well ...

... he's Joe.
Joe! Don't touch that.
I'll grab him.
I dunno about this, Sal ...
Douglas knows you. He'll listen to you. You're the only one who can stop him.
Come here, scallywag.
Well ... let's say I can stop Douglas. But you've only got one shot of shrink ray left! That means, once you shrink Douglas, I'll be stuck as a giant for days until you can collect more shrinky thingies, right?

With a few adjustments, I should be able to recalibrate the beam and shrink you both at the same time.
And you're sure it's the only way?
I'm sure. What do you say?
OK Sal. Let's do it.
That's the spirit!

Now Charli, just relax.
It's perfectly safe. The chance of your insides growing faster than your outsides and you popping like a human balloon is really quite low. One in 100 at the most. It worked on Douglas, so it should work on you.
Eeep!
EMBIGGENATING SEQUENCE ACTIVATED. TARGET ACQUIRED. FIRING IN 3 ...
Initiating!

2 ...
1 ...
... FIRE.
ZAP

Up ahead in
Runn Forest ...
AAAAAAAAAAAAAAAAAAAAaaaa
AAAAAAAAAAAAAAAA
AAAAAA
AAAAaa-

RUMBLE
GASP!
RUMBLE

RUMBLE
AAAAAAAAAAAAAAAAAAA

AAAAAAAAAAAAAAAAAA
AAAAAAAAAAAAAAAA
AAAAAAA

BOOT
AAAAAAAAAAAAAAAAAAA
CRASH!
AAAAAAAAAAAAAAAAAAAA

CRUNCH!
AA--

You're welcome!

AAAAAAAA

I hope Douglas is OK!
I'm sure he's fine. Quickly, put us down so we can prep the Resizenator.

OK.
You do
that ...
... I'll grab
Douglas.
Charli,
you've got
incoming!

BUMP
Hey!!
Nan, head
for the
turn-off.
Righto.

Douglas, no! That's a bad beetle.
Why don't you come up here where I can see you.

Goooood boy! Who's a good beetle, then? You've had a big day, huh?
How 'bout you come over this side, then your Aunty Sal can shrink us back down? Hmm?
Awwww! Sal, Ms Tinker, look!

He's giving his mum a hug!
So. Gross.
I've got a bad feeling about this.
Wha--

EEEP!
Eaton Squats Sewage Farm
Ovadah Hill 100m
Littleton 500m
CRUNCH

Douglas Archibald Stevenson!
She gave him a middle name?
Stop rolling that right now, mister.
Don't make me come over there.

Alright, that's it!

FWUMP
Now, stay put.
WHOA!

Uh ...

SALLYYYYYYY!

My hands are slipping!
Eaton Squats Sewage Farm
Ovadah Hill 100m
Littleton 500m
Hold on, Charli! Just a bit longer!

In a few moments we'll have a clear shot, so you'll be back to normal soon.
Unless, of course, the atoms that make you you - and Douglas Douglas - are accidentally mixed during the shrinkafication process ...

... in which case you'll turn into some kind of human / dung beetle mutant hybrid.
JUST PRESS THE BUTTON ALREADY!
Initiating!
SHRINKAFYING SEQUENCE ACTIVATED. TARGETS ACQUIRED. AUTO-DETECTING ORIGINAL SIZES. FIRING IN 3 ... 2 ... 1 ...

ZAP
... FIRE.

SHOOM
SHOOM
SHOOM
SHOOM
Eaton Squats Sewage Farm
Ovadah Hill 100m
Littleton 500m
Eaton Squats Sewage Farm
Ovadah Hill 100m
Littleton 500m
CHARLI!!

Sal!
We're back to normal!
Success!
Quit it, Joe, you're interrupting. What's so urgent?
Eaton Squats
Ovadah Hill
Oh.
Eaton Squats
Ovadah Hill

That.
Eaton Squats
Ovadah Hill
Littleto

What's the plan, Sal?
Yeah Sal, think!
Hang on ...
Eaton Squats
Ovadah Hill
Littleton
EMBIGGENATING SEQUENCE ACTIVATED.
... where's Joe?!
Eaton Squats
Ovadah Hill
Littleton
TARGET ACQUIRED.
FIRING IN 3 ... 2 ... 1 ...
ZAP
... FIRE.
Eaton Squats
Ovadah Hill
Littleton

Oh dung.

SHOOM
Eaton Squats
Ovadah Hill
Littleto

Meanwhile ...
clunk
clunk
clunk
RUMBLE
AAAAAAAAAAAA
And so ...

clunk
clunk
clunk
clunk
clunk
AAA
SPLOT
CREEEEAKK...

We're not out of the woods yet.
The dungball is, though.
So is Mr Eaton!

AAAAAAAAAAAA
Joe,
NO!
And so
is Joe!
AAAAAAAA

RUMBLE
AAAAAAAA

HOOM

AAAAAAAAAAAA

AAAAAAAAAAAAAAAAAA
SPLOTCH

Joe! You did it!
Poo.

Problem solved! Apart from this huge biohazard, of course.
That's not a nice thing to call your brother.
Ha-ha. Now all I have to do is collect more shrinkatrons, then I can shrink Joe AND the dungball.
But what if you don't shrink the ball? Could be a tourist attraction! 'Littleton: home of the Big Poo'.
Actually, that's not a bad idea.

So, how long will it take to fix the PLOT Device and collect more shrinky things?
Three days minimum.
Uh, Sal, your mum gets back from her yoga conference in two days.
Oh. You're right.
Can we tell her when she gets back?
Fine, but it's up to you to break the news, kiddo.

Have you figured out how you'll keep Joe occupied?
Simple. We'll embiggen his toys.
What about feeding him?
We'll embiggen his food too. Trust me, it will be fine.
I've already anticipated every outcome and formulated a foolproof plan. There's no problem Sally Tinker can't solve.

I'm glad you've figured it all out. And here I was about to ask how you're gonna change his nappies!
Uh ...

CLAP
CLAP
CLAP
CLAP
CLAP
sigh

THE END

Or is it?
Keep reading for a brilliant bonus story ...

ONE SMALL STEP FOR MAMMOTH

Greetings! I'm Sally Tinker, the world's foremost inventor under the age of twelve ...
... and soon to be the first Earthling on Mars!
My spaceship is the fastest ever built.
And I've got an incredible crew ...
S.TINKER INC.
SS. MARVIN
TOP VIEW
SIDE VIEW
CARGO BAY
FLIGHT DECK
S.TINKER INC
SS. MARVIN
FUSION-ASSISTED ROCKET THRUSTER ENGINES
HEAT SHIELDS

Charli Stevenson: biologist.
Rav Mitra: astrophysicist.
And my brother, Joe: baby.
So crew, are we ready for launch?

Aye aye, Captain Sal!
My veggie garden is safely onboard.
Rav's physics thingamajigs are all set up too.
Brilliant.
EARTH
MARS
SUN
Sal, according to my calculations ...
... Mars is in the optimal position for the next 3.27 hours.
EARTH
MARS
SUN

Then let's get going.
Joe, are you all packed?
Where's Baby Mammoth? Don't forget your favourite toy.
There it is!
We can't leave it behind ...
Wait, Joe. Where are you going ...

... oh boy.

Joe, you can't take a mammoth to Mars. Where did you even get an extinct animal?!
Sal, the TV!

Wally, a cloned woolly mammoth, was stolen from Maelstrom Corp last night.
21 DEC 5:02AM CAM 04
LAB
Security footage shows a short, chubby and quite adorable ninja freeing the mammoth.
21 DEC 5:02AM CAM 04
LAB
What the ...

SUSPECT

We're now live with police at the miniature ninja's hideout.
Oh crud.
Sal, that looks like your front door.
DANGER

KNOCK
KNOCK
KNOCK
KNOCK
KNOCK
KNOCK
DANGER
KEEP
OUT
It IS my front door!

Sally, it's Sergeant Salt and Constable Kipper. Open the door, please.
KEEP
OUT

Quick, everyone, into the Space Uniform Intuitive Tailoring chamber!
The what?
The S.U.I.T. Chamber. Hurry!
IN
It's ... a bit ... squeezy!
Now into the spaceship!

OUT
Wow, instant spacesuits!
Now into the lift!
Ping!

S.TINKER INC.
S.S. MARVIN
Where is Wally going to sit, Sal?

Here in the cargo bay. Can you strap him in?
Rav and Joe, follow me to the flight deck.
Aye aye, Captain.
Sally, we can't launch until we run final safety checks.
There's no time.
If the police find us packing that pachyderm, we'll be properly punished.

But what if the life support breaks down?
I'd be more worried about my experimental and highly explosive rocket fuel.
Tilting ship for vertical launch!
S.S. MARVIN
S.TINKER INC.
5 ...
4 ...
3 ...
2 ...
1 ...

Here in the cargo bay. Can you strap him in?
Rav and Joe, follow me to the flight deck.
Aye aye, Captain.

Sally, we can't launch until we run final safety checks.
There's no time.
If the police find us packing that pachyderm, we'll be properly punished.

But what if the life support breaks down?
I'd be more worried about my experimental and highly explosive rocket fuel.
Tilting ship for vertical launch!
S.S. MARVIN
S. TINKER INC.
5 ... 4 ... 3 ... 2 ... 1 ...

... blast off!
S.S. MARVIN
S. TINKER INC.
AAAARGH WE'RE ALL GONNA DIE!!

Later, in low Earth orbit ...
S.S. MARVIN
Rav, we're in space!
Isn't it all you ever wished for?
I wish I had a spare pair of space trousers.
I wish Joe had some too.

*Fusion-Assisted Rocket Thruster

Bad news, Sal.
What is it?

Well, Wally got a bit hungry after the launch ...

WALLY! You're eating all our food!

He didn't EAT it all ... he sat on my quinoa salad.
FOOD SUPPLY

CHOC
FOOD SUPPLY
He ate my veggie garden too! But it's not his fault.
We didn't bring enough food for three kids and a baby, PLUS a mammoth.
H2O
WASTE

Luckily we can do the round trip to Mars in 12 hours, so we won't starve.
It does mean cancelling our interplanetary picnic, but that's the way the cookie crumbles.
YOINK!
Rav, are your experiments still okay?
They're inedible, so they're fine.
Phew. Then it could have been worse ...
H_2O
WASTE

aaa ...
AAA ...
CHOO!
Oh crud.
SMASH

All my experiments ... crushed by a mammoth's bottom.
I'm beginning to think bringing a mammoth onto a spaceship was not a good idea ...
Uh oh, Sal. Wally needs to go to the bathroom!

No problem. This ship has the most high-tech space toilet ever built.
SPAAAAAAACE TOILET
I tested it under the worst conditions imaginable ...
... and by that I mean I let Joe use it.
He couldn't break it, so I doubt Wally could.

Sally, please think this through.
Yeah, Sal.
We all know Joe is very smelly compared to the average human ...

Okaaay ... in you go, Wally.

... but Wally is a woolly mammoth.
Oh please. I have full confidence in my space toilet. Let Wally do his worst.

CRUNCH!
FRRRRRRT POOT
PTHLTHB
SPLAT
KA-SPLASH
FLUSHHHHHHH

I stand corrected.
CLAP CLAP CLAP

So our food is finished, our experiments are extinct and our toilet is toast.
But things couldn't get any worse, right?

Saaaal! Whenever you say something like that, something worse happens.
That's not true! Is it, Rav?
It is when you say it.

I don't believe this ...
BEEP BEEP BEEP BEEP BEEP BEEP BEEP BEEP
... uh oh.

It's just an incoming shower of micrometeoroids.
What do we do?

It's just a bunch of tiny space rocks. I built the ship to withstand things like this.

PING
PING
PING
PING PING
PING
PING
PING
PING

See? It could've been much worse.
SAAAAL!

WHOOP WHOOP WHOOP WHOOP
This time it's a not-so-micro meteroid!
!!!
!!!
Everyone, helmets on NOW!
Brace for impact!
S.S. MARVIN

WHOOP WHOOP WHOOP WHOOP
Oh crud.
There's no time to change course.
It'll break a hole in the ship for sure!
!!!
Wally ... hold Joe tight for me.

Here it comes ...
S. TINKER INC.
BOOM
S. TINKER INC.

WHOOSH!
FOOD SUPPLY
I can't hold on much longer, Sal!

NO
NO
NO!

EEEK!
YEARGHHH!
NOOOO!

FOOD SUPPLY
JOE!

TUG
TUG
?
LEAP!

JOE! You're a lifesaver!
Almost ...
TWANG!
No, no, NO!

TUG
TUG

GRAB

HOORAY!

After a mammoth rescue effort, Sally patches up the ship ...

... and our heroes finally get to Mars!
Touch down!
Thank you for flying with S.Tinker Inc.
S.S. MARVIN
WHOOSH!

Crew, we've been through a lot to get here.
We lost our food, our experiments and our toilet ... and we almost lost our lives.
Three of us wouldn't even be here, if not for the bravery and quick thinking of my brother Joe and our newest crew member, Wally.

But now that we're finally here, the time has come for me to make history.
As your captain, it is my honour to be the first Earthling to set foot on --
Uh, Sal?

JOE! WALLY!
S.S. N

Thus ends another epic
S.Tinker Inc. adventure!

THE END

Want even MORE?
You're still in luck!
Check out my other awesome adventures - Chickensaurus, Gastronauts and Brobot!

< WHY DID HALF A CHICKEN CROSS THE ROAD? />
< TO GET TO ITS OTHER SIDE />

SALLY TINKER – THE WORLD'S FOREMOST INVENTOR UNDER TWELVE – IS FACING HER BIGGEST CHALLENGE YET.
WHEN SALLY'S ARCH-ENEMY INVITES HER TO A DEMONSTRATION OF HIS NEW INVENTION, SHE DOESN'T EXPECT IT TO ACTUALLY WORK. BUT IT DOES – DEXTER'S AMAZING DE-EVOLVING RAY CAN TURN CHICKENS INTO DINOSAURS!

WHEN THE CHICKENSAURS UNEXPECTEDLY BREAK FREE AND GO ON THE HUNT, SALLY FINDS HERSELF IN A DESPERATE RACE TO SAVE HER FRIENDS AND AVOID BECOMING CHICKEN FEED.

DID DEXTER HATCH THIS DASTARDLY PLOT – OR IS SOMEBODY ELSE THE BAD EGG?

Full of humour and witty puns on anything poultry, eggy or chickeny, kids will love the strength shown by Sally in leading her group to some sort of feathery end.

Magpies

JAMES FOLEY
IN ALL NEW FABULOUS COLOUR
CHICKEN-SAURUS

SALLY TINKER — THE WORLD'S FOREMOST INVENTOR UNDER THE AGE OF TWELVE — HAS DEVELOPED HER GREATEST INVENTION YET. BUT WHEN SALLY'S BABY BROTHER JOE SWALLOWS IT WITH DISASTROUS GASEOUS CONSEQUENCES, SALLY AND HER FRIEND CHARLI MUST SHRINK THEMSELVES, VENTURE INTO THE VERY BOWELS OF JOE, AND SHUT DOWN THE INVENTION BEFORE IT'S TOO LATE.

WHAT COULD POSSIBLY GO WRONG?

This graphic novel is hilariously funny. It will be devoured by newly independent and emerging readers.

Magpies

JAMES FOLEY
IN ALL NEW FABULOUS COLOUR
GASTRO-NAUTS

SALLY TINKER MAKES MACHINES ...

AND JOE TINKER BREAKS THEM.

AS THE WORLD'S FOREMOST INVENTOR UNDER THE AGE OF TWELVE, SALLY KNOWS SHE CAN BUILD A BETTER BROTHER THAN BABY JOE.

BUT IS HER INVENTION — BROBOT — REALLY ALL THAT A BROTHER SHOULD BE?

Brobot lives up to its promise as a hilarious graphic novel for young readers.

Buzz Words

JAMES FOLEY
IN ALL NEW FABULOUS COLOUR
BROBOT

This edition first published 2025 by
FREMANTLE PRESS

Fremantle Press Inc. trading as Fremantle Press
PO Box 158, North Fremantle, Western Australia, 6159
fremantlepress.com.au

Dungzilla was first published by Fremantle Press in 2017.
The original version of 'One Small Step for Mammoth' first appeared in
The School Magazine, 2021.

Designed by James Foley and Rebecca Mills, rebeccamills.com.au
Dungzilla colourisation by Paulina Gamez
Printed by Everbest Printing Investment Limited, China

A catalogue record for this book is available from the National Library of Australia

ISBN 9781760993368 (paperback)
ISBN 9781760993795 (ebook)

Department of Local Government, Sport and Cultural Industries | lotterywest

Fremantle Press is supported by the State Government through the Department of Local Government, Sport and Cultural Industries.

Fremantle Press respectfully acknowledges the Whadjuk people of the Noongar nation as the Traditional Owners and Custodians of the land where we work in Walyalup.

MIX
From responsible sources
FSC® C124385